© 2012 Disney Enterprises, Inc.
Published by Hachette Partworks Ltd.
ISBN: 978-1-908648-39-6
Date of Printing: April 2012
Printed in Malaysia by Tien Wah Press

THE LION KING 3
HAKUNA MATATA

THE GREAT FLOOD

Disney

Hachette

Once, there was a young lion cub named Simba.
His best friends were Timon, a little meerkat,
and a big warthog called Pumbaa. The thing they
enjoyed doing most was... nothing!

One day, after a big lunch of wiggly worms and crunchy grubs, Simba's friends rested on the river bank while Simba studied the clouds.

The cub scratched his head. "I think the cloud shapes mean something," he said. "I wish I could figure out what."

Timon yawned. "Why bother when there's so much sleeping to do?"

"Maybe clouds can tell you about the weather," said Pumbaa. "You know, whether it's going to rain or not."

"Do you think they can?" wondered Simba.

"What?" Timon looked up. "That's the silliest thing I've ever heard!"

The meerkat laughed and laughed.
"You don't have to look at clouds to know
the weather."

"When you see the sun, it's a sunny day. Or just stick out your paw. If it gets wet, it's raining," Timon told them.

Pumbaa smiled. "You're probably right," he said, as he wandered off for a swim.

"Is that really all there is to it, Timon?" asked Simba.

"Of course," said Timon, sticking out his paw. "You see? It isn't raining."

Just then, Pumbaa jumped into the river. *SPLASH!*

Timon was soaked!

"Hey, Timon!" called Pumbaa. "Your paw's wet now. Is it raining?" The warthog laughed so hard that his big belly made big ripples in the water.

Simba laughed, too. But Timon didn't.

"I'm right" insisted Timon. "When your paw gets wet, then it's raining."

"Right," agreed Pumbaa. "So it must be raining now."

And Pumbaa and Simba laughed again.

The friends went back to their sleeping spot on the river bank.

"Nothing like a refreshing shower – right, Timon?" said Pumbaa. The little meerkat didn't answer.

Simba stretched out. The sun warmed his fur. He yawned and said, "I can learn to understand clouds later." And he fell asleep.

Before long, a young giraffe called Bahati
woke them up. "It's time to play," she called.
    "Let's play Slide'n'Bounce," suggested
Pumbaa.
    Timon and Simba took turns sliding down
Bahati's long neck and bouncing off Pumbaa
into the river.

Bahati had some news. "My mother is having a baby. Soon, I'll have a little brother or sister," she announced.

"That's great!" Timon cried. "Then we'll have two slides!"

The friends had lots of fun. They didn't notice the dark clouds filling the sky.

Suddenly, it was as dark as night.
Thunder boomed! Lightning flashed!
"Yikes!" cried Pumbaa.
"Run for cover!" shouted Timon, as torrents
of rain started pouring down from the sky.

As the friends
huddled together,
Simba noticed that the
river was rising higher
and higher. It was
about to burst its banks!
    "We must move to
higher ground," said
Simba to his friends.

The four friends ran for the hills. Lots of other animals had decided to do the same thing.

Bahati looked for her mother in the crowd, but she couldn't find her.

The young giraffe suddenly stopped running. "What if my mother needs help?" she asked, looking worried.

"Where could your mother be?" asked Simba.

"The last time I saw her, she was down by the river," replied Bahati.

"Well then, let's go!" said Simba.

The storm was getting worse as the friends turned round and headed back to the river. The wind bent the trees almost to the ground.

"Help! I'm a meer-kite!" wailed Timon as he clung on to Pumbaa's tail.

Just then, a hippopotamus lumbered up to Bahati. "Your mother is trapped on an island further up river," cried the hippo. "The water's too high – none of us can reach her!"

The four friends rushed off and soon found Bahati's mother, Sukari. The flood waters raged all around the tiny island. It was impossible for her to escape!

"What can we do?" sobbed Bahati.

"We'll never be able to swim out to her. We'd need fins!" shrieked Timon.

"Or wings," added Pumbaa.

But Simba had an idea. "We can make a raft!" he declared.

The friends quickly got to work.
Bahati found some vines.
Timon and Pumbaa gathered
fallen tree trunks.

Simba kept an
eye on the river. It
was rising fast. They
would have to hurry!

Tying the trunks together was hard work, but by working as a team, the friends soon finished building their raft.

They pushed the raft into the water. Simba
and Bahati climbed aboard.

"Hang on!" Simba shouted as the raft
bounced and dipped in the wild water.

Bahati cried, "Oh no! We're going to float past the island!"

"There's only one thing to do," said Simba. He took one end of a vine between his teeth. The other end was tied to the raft. Then the brave young cub jumped into the water.

Simba swam to the island. He started to clamber onto the shore, but the river's strong current pulled him back. He began to slip back into the water!

Quickly, Sukari stretched down her long neck and pulled Simba to safety.

Together, Simba and Sukari pulled the raft to the island.

Bahati and Sukari were so happy to see
each other!
Soon, the two giraffes were safely on the
raft. Then Simba jumped aboard, too.

The little raft pitched up and down on the raging flood waters.

"Watching all that bouncing is making me feel seasick," said Timon nervously.

Finally, the raft reached dry land safely.

But their troubles weren't over yet!
"My baby is coming soon," said Sukari.
"There's a cave near here," said Timon.
"You could go there."
The clouds were starting to clear. "I think
it will stop raining soon," said Simba. He was
beginning to understand clouds!

Bahati's mother went into the cave. The friends waited anxiously outside.

Other animals came to the cave. They wanted to welcome the baby giraffe, too.

Simba felt guilty.

"It's all my fault," he said. "If I had learned to understand clouds sooner, I would have known the storm was coming. Then your mother would never have been trapped on the island."

"But it was you who *saved* my mother!" replied
Bahati. "You were so brave, Simba! You'll be a
great lion one day."

"And you're already a good friend," Pumbaa told
him. Timon nodded in agreement.

Just then, the air filled with joyful sounds as the
animals around the cave started cheering!

The friends found Sukari with her new baby.
"Bahati, meet your brother," said Sukari.
Bahati smiled. "Can he come out to play?" she
asked her mother.

Sukari laughed. "Not yet – he has to learn how to walk first!"

Sukari turned to Simba. "You are a brave lion," she said. "Thank you for saving us."

The animals left the mother and
baby to rest.

"This calls for a celebration!"
announced Timon. "Grubs for
everyone!"

But Simba wasn't listening. He
was too busy studying the sky.

"I have to watch the clouds to make
sure it isn't going to rain again," he said.

"There isn't a cloud in the sky," Timon pointed out. Simba looked up. His friend was right.

"Besides," continued Timon, "it's definitely not going to rain. Look – my paw isn't wet."

Just as he held his paw out to Simba, Pumbaa jumped into the river with a huge SPLASH!

"Looks like rain to me, Timon!" chuckled Simba.

"What... why...?" spluttered Timon. Then he looked at his friends, who were all roaring with laughter.

"I guess when it rains, it boars," said Timon with a shrug. "Hakuna matata!"
And with that, he joined in the laughter, too!